# A DREAMING INSOMNIAC

AKASH RAJA D S

Made with ♥ on the Notion Press Platform
www.notionpress.com

I dedicate this book to all the readers who enjoy getting confused or surprised. I truly believe there's a whole tribe of people like me who love the thrill of a good brain teaser. After all, without confusion, where would magic and magicians be, right? So, here it is—my first book, my dream, and my little whirlwind of a confusing story—dedicated to you wonderful folks. Enjoy the chaos!

# Contents

# Preface

**"A Dreaming Insomniac"** is a fictional drama unfolds across two gripping, non-linear timelines, weaving the lives of two unique characters, Sudeep and Maadhavan, into a surreal tapestry of dreams and reality.

In one storyline, we meet **Sudeep**, a man plagued by relentless insomnia. Nights stretch endlessly as sleep evades him, casting a shadow on his waking life. Desperate for relief, he turns to the enigmatic Dr. RamSingh, a psychiatrist with a twist—he's 300 years old and armed with both centuries of wisdom and a groundbreaking dream-manipulation technology. Together, they embark on a journey into the depths of Sudeep's subconscious, battling the chaos within to restore the harmony of sleep.

In the parallel storyline, we follow **Maadhavan**, an 18-year-old school student caught in the throes of a crucial—and increasingly surreal—situation. As the lines between the possible and the impossible blur, Maadhavan experiences a jarring revelation: he's inside a dream. This realization hits hard when elements of his waking life seep into his subconscious, bending the rules of his fabricated world and forcing him to question the boundaries of reality itself.

Two lives. Two dreams. A shared exploration of the mysteries within. *A Dreaming Insomniac* invites you to dive deep into a story where perception twists, reality bends, and the mind reigns supreme.

# Acknowledgements

First and foremost, I extend my heartfelt thanks to my dear friend, Citrarasu. Citrarasu and I were classmates during our undergraduate days, and our journeys home on the train were filled with endless conversations about movies and short films. It was during those train rides that we dreamed up countless ideas, including the genesis of The Dreaming Insomniac.

I want to extend my deepest gratitude to my beloved person, the one who stands by me unconditionally and encourages me no matter what.

I also want to thank all my friends for their unwavering support throughout this journey. Finally, my deepest gratitude goes to my parents, whose love and guidance have shaped me into the person I am today. Thank you all for being a part of this dream

# Prologue

*"Should I end it like this...? Something's missing. It's just not hitting the emotional note I want... Aahhh, I have no clue how to wrap this up. What should I do? I need a break. Yes, maybe a break will help"* Maadhavan murmured, his voice tinged with frustration.

The rain lashed against the windows, the sound echoing through the quiet, dimly lit room. The downpour was relentless, the kind that often left Chennai in darkness, as it had now. Power outages were a familiar inconvenience, but tonight it felt like an added weight.

Eighteen-year-old Maadhavan sat cross-legged on his bed, the edges of his writing pad digging into his thighs. His script papers fluttered slightly in the cool breeze seeping through the open windows. The air smelled of wet earth and carried a faint chill, a contrast to the heat that usually blanketed the city.

He had been pouring his heart into this script for weeks now, crafting the story with care and passion. The short film was meant to be their magnum opus, something he, Abdullah, and Jeeva could submit proudly for the competition just three months away. The beginning flowed effortlessly, the middle had shaped up beautifully, but the climax? It was his nemesis.

Every time he thought he had it, it slipped through his fingers like sand. The emotional punch he sought felt distant and unattainable. He clenched his pen, tapping it against his head as if the motion could dislodge the perfect ending from his thoughts.

Unable to sit still any longer, he grabbed his phone and dialed Abdullah. The phone rang, its peculiar ringtone cutting through the sound of rain.

*"Hello, Maadhavan?"* Abdullah's voice crackled on the line.

*"Where are you? I'm stuck, man. I can't get the climax right. It's driving me insane"* Maadhavan blurted out, his voice fraught with tension.

*"Relax da. Jeeva and I are out shopping for the costumes. We'll be back in an hour. Just hang in there"* Abdullah replied, trying to soothe him. "I'll bring samosas. Take a break till we get back."

The call ended, but the tightness in Maadhavan's chest remained. He placed the phone down and wandered into the kitchen. He filled a glass of water and stared out of the window, watching the rain cascade in shimmering sheets. The thought of the competition deadline gnawed at him.

*"Three months"* he whispered to himself, the weight of the timeline pressing down on him. There was so much to do: rehearsals, shooting, music composition, editing. How could they pull it off when he couldn't even finish the script?

Determined not to wait, he returned to his bed and stared at the blank page. His pen hovered over the paper, but the words wouldn't come. Every idea felt wrong, every attempt fell flat. Frustrated, he slammed the pad onto the bed and leaned back, pressing his hands against his face.

The rain outside seemed to grow heavier, mirroring the storm within him. For a moment, he closed his eyes and let the sound of the rain envelop him. His breath hitched as an overwhelming mix of exhaustion and hopelessness coursed through him.

*"What's wrong with me?"* he muttered, staring at the ceiling. The room felt colder now, and despite his frustration, a pang of loneliness settled in his chest. He

needed to believe that he could do this—that the story he carried within him could come alive.

But at that moment, all he felt was the crushing weight of doubt.

# I

# I Am Insomniac

In the dead of night, 10-year-old Sudeep was abruptly woken by the sound of his mother's desperate cries from the adjacent room. His heart pounding, he crept to the window and peered through it. The sight that met his eyes was horrifying: his father stood menacingly, a kitchen knife gripped in his right hand, while his left hand choked Sudeep's mother. She tried to resist, pleading, *"No... please don't kill me, please... don't..."*

Frozen with fear, Sudeep's tears flowed silently, his hands muffling his cries. Suddenly, his father's head turned, his eyes locking onto Sudeep's. Paralyzed with dread, Sudeep stumbled backward, uncovering his mouth. His mother's screams grew more frantic, but they were abruptly silenced as his father began to stab her repeatedly. Her voice weakened and faded, leaving Sudeep in stunned silence. He pressed his hands tightly over his ears, sobbing uncontrollably. Despite his attempts to block out the horror, a voice pierced through his thoughts, *"Hey Sudeep... Sudeep, wake up, man."*

With a jolt, Sudeep awoke at his office desk. His boss, Sandy, was shaking him awake, shouting, *"Sudeep, wake up... Can you hear me? Sudeep?"* Realizing he had fallen asleep at work yet again, Sudeep rubbed his eyes, looking up with a sorrowful expression. "Sorry, Sandy, I'm really sorry! I fell asleep again..."

Annoyed, Sandy retorted, *"This is the third time this week. You should not sleep like this at the workplace. If you want to sleep, just leave and sleep at home."*

Sudeep apologized once more, assuring Sandy it wouldn't happen again. Sandy sighed, *"If you can't sleep at night, go and consult another psychiatrist, but don't sleep here,"* before walking away.

Shaking off the remnants of his nightmare, Sudeep trudged to the coffee machine to refill his cup. As he poured the coffee, memories of his past swirled in his mind.

Lost in thought, he didn't notice the coffee overflowing until it spilled over. Hastily turning off the machine, he took his cup and returned to his desk, sipping his coffee and diving back into his design work while continuing his blog titled **"I AM INSOMNIAC."**

*"Hi, I'm Sudeep. I am a 26-year-old structural engineer working at Ultra-Strong Foundations, and I am an insomniac. It is a condition where a person cannot sleep effectively. I developed this condition due to overstress and overthinking my past tragedies.*

*When I was 10, my father killed my mother and then hung himself. After that incident, I was admitted to an orphanage, where I completed my schooling. I graduated in civil engineering from Oletech Engineering College with a 90% scholarship.*

*Then I joined a construction company as a site engineer. There, I met Chandru. After a few years of work, we both started our own company. I invested all my savings and assets into the start-up, but within a year, Chandru started to cheat me by paying me only a small percentage of the profit, much less than my previous salary. So, I decided to withdraw my partnership with the company. Since we didn't sign any legal partnership agreement, he didn't pay back my full investment. He beguiled me, and I received only half of my investment.*

*After that, I joined Ultra-Tech Foundations. I've been working here for almost two years, and this is where I met Pallavi. Pallavi is the most beautiful girl I have ever met. If being so beautiful were a crime, she would be the most wanted criminal in the world. She had magnetic eyes that attracted me. Only after meeting her did I learn the language that everyone on earth can understand in their hearts—it was love. I loved her and decided to marry her. I proposed to her, and luckily, she accepted my proposal. She was the only perfect thing that happened in my life, but it didn't last long. One day, she suddenly broke up with me and married someone her parents had arranged.*

*That's when the frustration developed. Love can break more than the heart—it can shatter the mind. I didn't sleep for almost three days, thinking about why Pallavi accepted my love in the first place, why she broke up with me, and why she married someone else. Was it because I didn't have enough money to make her happy? Was she afraid to tell her parents about our relationship? Or was there another reason for the breakup? And why did Chandru cheat me?*

*I trusted him more than anyone else in this world. He was my only friend, but he too cheated me. And why did my father kill my mother? Why did he hang himself? Why did they give birth to me? If they were alive, I would undoubtedly file a case against them for bringing me into this hideous world. There were so many questions in my mind. Should I commit suicide? What if I die tomorrow? There would be no one to mourn for me. I don't know why I was born, and I have no idea what I am going to do next in my life. The stress in my head increased like COVID-19 cases in India. That's when I developed insomnia. I overstressed myself by constantly thinking about these incidents and didn't sleep productively for a week.*

*Only a week later did I realize I was suffering from insomnia. I couldn't sleep at night, and then I would fall asleep during the day. I didn't know when, where, or how much I was sleeping. I mostly slept only 2-3 hours a day. I tried using sleeping pills, but they only made the situation worse. I also tried YouTube remedies for insomnia, but they ended in failure. After that, I consulted a doctor. The doctor told me to do a few exercises at night before sleeping, and he also conducted sleeping sessions twice a week. I attended these sessions for three months and noticed improvement. It almost cured me. But since last week, I stopped going there because I don't have enough money to pay for those sessions. That doctor charges 5000 rupees for each session, which is why I stopped going. I continued doing the night sleeping exercises, but they didn't help me sleep anymore. This week, I got caught sleeping three times during work hours. If I sleep again during work, my boss, Sandy, will fire me. Indeed, he is a good human being. He knows about my condition and gave me permission to attend those sessions. Yet, if I get caught next time, he will fire me for sure. As Sandy told me, I must consult another psychiatrist, or the situation will become worse.*"

Sudeep saved and published his blog and then started doing his office work.

After work, Sudeep went straight home. He sat in front of his laptop and started searching for a psychiatrist near him. While exploring the internet, his eyes caught something weird: **A 300-year-old psychiatrist, Dr. RamSingh, giving free lectures to improve interpersonal qualities.** It surprised Sudeep. *"How can someone live up to 300 years?"*

At first, he thought it might be a typing error, fake news, or a kind of fake promotion. But he searched more about Dr. RamSingh and found that he was truly 300 years old. He also read an article about Dr. RamSingh's biography and learned that the doctor got this long-living ability due to an accident that occurred in his 40s. Sudeep became curious to meet him and thought this man could cure his condition.

Sudeep searched for a clinic or hospital where Dr. RamSingh was working. Sadly, Sudeep learned that two years ago, the hospital where the doctor worked caught fire.

After that incident, he stopped giving therapies and lectures. But fortunately, Sudeep found the doctor's house address in one of the articles. He called Sandy, told him about the psychiatrist, and asked for permission to take leave from work to meet the psychiatrist.

Sandy gave him permission to consult the psychiatrist. So, Sudeep planned to meet the psychiatrist the next morning.

# II

# Maadhavan Wake up!!! – Part 1

The rain roared against the windows, a relentless cascade from the heavens that seemed determined to drown the world. Maadhavan lay snug under his blanket, the rhythm of the storm lulling him into a deep, undisturbed slumber. But his peace was shattered when a thunderclap, as loud as a cannon blast, shook the very walls of his home. His eyes flew open, and he sat upright, heart pounding.

The clock read 7:00 AM. Through the rain-spattered glass, he could see the downpour outside, relentless and unyielding. He sighed, deciding that school could wait; this weather called for nothing more than a cozy, extended nap. But first, nature's call demanded attention.

Groggily, Maadhavan shuffled to the toilet. He finished, flushed, and washed his hands.

As he reached to turn off the light, a cold droplet of water splashed onto his wrist. He froze, looking up to see a dark stain on the ceiling, water seeping through it.

*"Maa! Rainwater is leaking near the toilet! Bring a bowl, maa!"* he shouted, his voice laced with urgency.

From the other room, his mother's voice came, tinged with confusion. *"What? Water is leaking? We're on the ground floor of a three-story building. How can it rain inside?"*

Her words gave him pause. She was right—it didn't make sense. "Maybe the neighbors..." he began, but before he could finish, more leaks erupted, water streaming in from the ceiling in multiple places.

Within moments, the entire house seemed to dissolve into chaos, with rain pouring inside as if the walls and roof had vanished.

*"Maa, what is happening?"* Maadhavan yelled, his voice a mix of fear and amazement. He received no answer. Alarmed, he hurried to the kitchen, expecting to find his mother.

But the kitchen was eerily empty. His breath hitched as he spotted someone else standing there—his math teacher.

*"Sir... what are you doing here? Where is my mom?"* he stammered, confusion etched across his face.

The teacher's gaze was steady, his voice deep and commanding as he said, *"Maadhavan... wake up."*

Something shifted in Maadhavan. His pupils widened as realization dawned. *"Am I dreaming?"* he thought, his surroundings beginning to blur and fade.

With a jolt, Maadhavan awoke to the sound of raucous laughter. He blinked rapidly, his head snapping up from his desk. He was back in his classroom, and his classmates were in stitches, pointing at him.

Standing beside him, holding a water bottle, was his math teacher, his expression a mixture of irritation and disappointment.

It all clicked. Maadhavan groaned inwardly as he realized he had fallen asleep—again—in the middle of math class.

೮೦

**<u>Half an hour earlier</u>**

*"Maadhavan,"* the principal had said sternly, *"your math teacher tells me you're constantly dozing off in class. This is your final warning. If it happens again, I'll have no choice but to call your parents."*

*"I promise, sir, it won't happen again"* Maadhavan had assured, his voice full of resolve.

Returning to class, Maadhavan had been determined to stay awake. At first, he listened attentively as the teacher explained the mysteries of trigonometry. But soon, the enthusiasm waned. The classroom fell silent except for the droning voice of his teacher. The blackboard was filled with equations and diagrams that felt like a foreign language to Maadhavan.

The weight of boredom pressed down on him. His eyelids grew heavy, his vision blurred, and the steady monotony of the teacher's voice became a lullaby. Try as he might, he couldn't resist the pull of sleep. Slowly, he leaned forward, his head resting on his desk as he succumbed to slumber.

And now, here he was—soaked from his teacher's water bottle, the laughter of his peers ringing in his ears, and the realization of his broken promise sinking heavily into his chest.

# III

# Kopi Luwak

Sudeep stood outside the door of Dr. RamSingh's house, hesitating to knock. What if the doctor refused to treat him? What if he couldn't be cured? With trepidation, he knocked on the door.

He heard footsteps approaching, and the door opened to reveal a middle-aged man, around 55 years old, with a grey beard and moustache, wearing a white kurta and a turban. The man asked, *"Who are you?"*

*"Hi... I'm Sudeep, and I'm looking for Dr. RamSingh"* Sudeep replied. The man responded, *"I am RamSingh. Why are you here? If you need medical help, I'm sorry, but I may not be able to help you."*

Sudeep paused, then impulsively replied, *"Doctor, I really need your help."*

Dr. RamSingh, who hadn't practiced in two years, explained, *"Sudeep, right? I stopped giving treatment two years ago. Don't waste your time here; consult someone else who can certainly cure you."*

Sudeep, without hesitation, said, *"I've seen many doctors, but none could cure me. I believe you are the only one who can help me. Please, doctor..."* Dr. RamSingh thought for a moment and asked, *"What disease are you suffering from?"* Sudeep replied that he was an insomniac.

Curious, the doctor decided to give it a try. *"Okay, Sudeep, I'll try my best, but I can't assure you that I will cure you completely."* Sudeep thanked him, and the doctor invited him into the living room.

Dr. RamSingh asked Sudeep to sit on the sofa while he went to the kitchen to make coffee. A few minutes later, the doctor returned with a cup of coffee in one hand and a bulky book in the other. He handed the cup to Sudeep, placed the book on the teapoy, and retrieved a device resembling an Xbox 360 with two headphones from his bedroom. Sitting down, he asked, *"Sudeep, tell me about yourself and how you got insomnia."* Sudeep sipped his coffee and began sharing his troubled life and the incidents that led to his sleeplessness.

After finishing his story and coffee, Sudeep placed the empty cup on the teapoy. The doctor asked, *"So, you think your life is terrible, and that's why you have this condition, right?"* Sudeep replied, *"Yes, doctor. If my life were perfect, I wouldn't be an insomniac."*

The doctor took a deep breath and asked, *"How was the coffee?"* Sudeep said, *"It's good. It's one of the finest coffees I've ever had."* The doctor smiled, came closer, and asked, *"Do you know what that coffee was made of?"* Sudeep replied, *"Milk, sugar, and coffee powder, right?"*

*"Yes, but the coffee you drank was made from the world's costliest coffee powder, KOPI LUWAK: coffee beans digested by an Indonesian cat breed"* the doctor said with a chuckle. Sudeep looked puzzled. *"Really? From cat poop? Are you serious? But it tasted like normal coffee; in fact, it tasted better than my usual coffee."*

*"I'm not bluffing. It's truly made from cat feces and is the world's most expensive coffee. Isn't that strange? Humans have the remarkable ability to turn even cat waste into a delicious, high-priced beverage. Similarly, you can turn your difficult life into a perfect one. You have full control over your life. Our mind is like a fragile glass pot; once it's broken into pieces, we can't restore its original shape by gluing the shattered pieces together, but we can create a new, better one by melting the broken fragments. You must try to burn down your past memories, relax your mind, and start anew"* the doctor explained.

Sudeep agreed. *"Okay, doctor, I'll try to forget my past and relax my thoughts."* The doctor took the bulky notebook and began leafing through the pages. Observing him, Sudeep hesitantly asked, *"Doctor, can I ask you a question?"*

The doctor closed the book, set it aside, and turned towards Sudeep. *"Go ahead"* he said. Sudeep continued, *"Are you really 300 years old? You don't look that old. You seem to be in your 50s or 60s. How did you get this ability?"* The doctor leaned forward and replied, *"Yes, I am 302 years old. This isn't an ability or superpower; it's a disease, a condition like yours."*

Sudeep chuckled, *"Disease! I see it as a gift—living like an eternal, an immortal."* The doctor responded, *"No, Sudeep, it's not like that. I'm not immortal. I will die one day; my aging ability has just diminished."* Sudeep disagreed, *"But how can you call it a disease? You can live longer than anyone in this world, right?"*

*"Not exactly. I'm the 50th person in the world with this condition, but almost everyone else killed themselves. I'm the only one still alive with this disease"* the doctor replied. Sudeep was puzzled, *"Why did they commit suicide?"*

The doctor took a deep breath and asked, *"Would you genuinely feel happy living 300 years with insomnia?"*

*"No... but without insomnia, I would gladly live for 300 years"* Sudeep admitted.

The doctor shook his head, *"Now tell me, which incident in your life affected you the most?"* Sudeep answered, *"My mom's death... and breaking up with Pallavi."*

The doctor expected that answer. *"See, the hardest thing is forgetting the one you love the most. If you lose someone you love, it pains a lot, right? If you live 300 years, you'll have to see your parents die, your friends die, your spouse and children die, and it will keep happening. No one can bear that pain, and that's why they all committed suicide."* Sudeep realized the truth in the doctor's words. *"That's right, doctor. No one can bear that much pain."*

Sudeep paused, then asked, *"Sorry to ask, but why didn't you commit suicide?"* The doctor laughed, *"Because I promised my wife. I got this condition during a ship accident in the Atlantic. Almost everyone on the ship died that night, including my wife and children. Only a few were saved using lifeboats. I was rescued after three hours in minus 25 degrees Celsius water. The cold damaged my aging cells, specifically the GATA6 gene, which is why I'm aging so slowly. That night, I promised my wife I wouldn't die or commit suicide until I got old. That's why I'm still here, keeping my promise."* Sudeep felt sorry for him. *"Right, doctor. We all have to keep our promises"* he replied with a fabricated smile.

The doctor picked up the book again and showed it to Sudeep. *"This is my diary, my 300 years of experience. I've done many things in my life. I've been a family man, a lecturer, a psychiatrist. I've also committed murder and was imprisoned for 35 years"* the doctor revealed. Sudeep was astonished, his eyes wide. The doctor continued, *"In prison, I learned how to face life and handle stress. After that, I studied psychology and became a psychiatrist. My therapies are like 'Q & A sessions.' I ask you a question, and you answer. You ask me a question, and I answer. It's like an effortless conversation, but not here..."*

"Not here? Do we have to go somewhere for the therapy?" Sudeep asked.

*"Yes, we both are going to my dream"* the doctor replied, expecting further questions from Sudeep. Sudeep was confused, *"Your dream? Really... 'A Dream World'... can you do that?"* The doctor showed the device on the teapoy and said, *"Yes, I can. See that? That is 'MY_DREAM_DEVICE' (MDD), a device to manipulate dreams. One of my friends, Cobb, lives in France. He gave me that device. It emits electromagnetic waves at a certain frequency, causing the brain to release melatonin and oxytocin, which induce sleep and dreams."*

Sudeep was still confused but accepted that the doctor could control dreams. However, he still had a question, *"Okay, doctor, but why do we need this? Why in a dream?"*

*"Well, implanting an idea in a dream will have more impact than in reality. For example, a nightmare frightens you more than a horror film, right?"* Sudeep nodded, and the doctor continued, *"And the impact of that nightmare lasts longer than the horror film. Similarly, therapy in a dream will have more impact than in reality. That's why I use this device in my therapies. Are you ready for this?"*

*"I'm not sure, but I hope this works for me. Let's do this"* Sudeep replied doubtfully. The doctor gave the blue headset to Sudeep and asked him to wear it. He wore the red headset himself and switched on the device, saying, *"Okay, Sudeep, let's get into my dream."*

# IV

# Maadhavan wake up!!! – Part 2

Maadhavan woke up abruptly in his classroom, realizing that he had once again dozed off during his math class. As his classmates laughed, the teacher silenced them and instructed Maadhavan to stand. He quickly stood and apologized, but the teacher ignored him and ordered him to stand outside the classroom. Without a word, Maadhavan walked out and stood near the door. A few minutes later, he peeked inside to see what his friends were doing. His friend Abdullah noticed him and gave a reassuring smile, which Maadhavan returned before resuming his position outside.

Maadhavan stood outside the classroom, his patience stretched thin as he waited for the class to end. The muffled sounds of the teacher's lecture filtered through the door, blending with the distant hum of school activity. Just as he began to lose himself in thought, a faint but distinct sound reached his ears—the steady echo of footsteps ascending the stairs, He glanced at his watch; it was 12:15 PM, just

15 minutes before lunch break. Then, he remembered that the principal always made rounds to monitor classes before lunch. Panic set in. *"What if the principal sees me? He'll ask why I'm outside and find out I slept in class again. There's no warning this time—he'll call my father for sure. I'm so dead. It's okay if my dad hits me, but he won't. He'll torture me with endless advice,"* he thought.

Nervously, Maadhavan began to sweat. He prayed that the person coming up the stairs wasn't the principal, but his fears were confirmed as the principal ascended and spotted him.

The principal furiously approached, and Maadhavan, frightened, turned his head to the right to see if the principal was really coming. When he looked back, Abdullah was standing right in front of him, upright like a military officer.

Shocked, Maadhavan stumbled back and asked, *"Abdul... what are you doing here? Why are you staring at me like a ghost?"* In a deep voice, Abdullah replied, *"Maadhavan... wake up."* Confused, Maadhavan looked back at the principal, who was now shouting in a vendor's tone, *"Samosa... hot samosa... samosee..."* Maadhavan felt a surge of panic; his principal was selling samosas, and his best friend was giving him a terrifying look while ordering him to wake up. Overwhelmed, he covered his ears. Moments later, he removed his hands and looked at Abdullah in surprise. His pupils dilated as he realized he was dreaming. "This is a dream too?" he thought.

Maadhavan awoke in a bus. Abdullah sat next to him, trying to wake him up, while a samosa vendor yelled outside.

☙

## **<u>Half an hour earlier:</u>**

At the bustling Chennai Koyambedu Bus Stand, Maadhavan and Abdullah had been waiting patiently for their bus. Abdullah, excited to spend the vacation in his native village near Hyderabad, had invited Maadhavan to join him, a plan eagerly approved by Maadhavan's parents.

When their bus finally arrived, the pair boarded and settled into their reserved seats. Maadhavan took the window seat, enjoying the view of the crowded station. Abdullah, ever the thoughtful friend, bought two packets of biscuits and handed one to Maadhavan.

As they munched, Abdullah grinned. *"The bus will stop at Furfuri Nagar. You have to try the mutton samosas there—they're amazing!"*

*"Yeah, sure"* Maadhavan replied with a wide yawn. *"Just make sure you wake me up if I fall asleep."*

The bus began its journey, merging onto the highway. Abdullah slipped on his headphones, nodding along to his music, while Maadhavan stretched his legs and leaned his head against the cool glass. The rhythmic vibrations of the bus lulled him into a deep, uninterrupted sleep—until the dream world came crashing in.

# V
# Lucid

Sudeep and Dr. RamSingh walked down the corridor of a hotel, flanked by doors bearing different numbers. As they strolled, Dr. RamSingh initiated a conversation, *"Okay Sudeep, what do you usually visualize while you lay on your bed?"*

Sudeep sighed, *"Mostly, I think about my past. Why did that incident happen to me? Why did I react like that? What would have happened if I had reacted differently? Things like that."*

Dr. RamSingh nodded thoughtfully, *"Alright, let me remind you once again; life will become simpler only when you let go of the baggage of your past. You must gain control over your thoughts. Your happiness entirely depends on the quality of your thoughts, so always feed your mind with positivity and happiness, or don't feed it at all. As Palak Rawat said, 'Sometimes a blank mind is better than negative thoughts.'"*

*"But doctor, how can I keep my thoughts empty?"* Sudeep asked, puzzled.

*"By living in the present. Only when you live in the present can you keep your thoughts empty. Try to avoid thinking about*

*anything except the task at hand. Every stressed person has difficulty keeping their mind in the present; they always struggle to concentrate on one job because their mind drifts back to the past. But with a few exercises, you can develop the ability to focus on the present. One of the best ways is to concentrate on your breath. Here's your first exercise: simply sit in a chair or lie on your bed and try to focus only on your breathing for at least 15 minutes."*

"Only 15 minutes? That sounds easy," Sudeep remarked.

"Concentrating solely on breathing is not as easy as it sounds. Your mind may wander. Note how many times you get distracted by various thoughts during those 15 minutes. Do this exercise regularly before sleep and monitor your progress. As I mentioned, this is the first and simplest step, but it's an effective one. If you observe a decrease in distractions over time, it means you're healing," Dr. RamSingh explained.

"Okay, doctor. I'll give it a try. But where am I? What is this place? Where are we going?" Sudeep asked skeptically.

"We are in a 'DREAM' simulated by me. This hotel, this environment—all were created by my imagination. I call this place 'LUCID,' a path that connects 'Deep_dream' and 'reality.' Here, you'll be aware that you're dreaming, but once you enter 'Deep_dream,' you won't recognize it as a dream. The dream will feel like reality. You can experience all the emotions, pain, happiness, sadness—everything."

"Okay, how do we get there?" Sudeep asked curiously.

"To enter 'Deep_dream,' we must go... there," Dr. RamSingh replied, pointing to a door about ten feet away.

They approached the door labeled 'MY DREEM' instead of a room number. Dr. RamSingh opened it and signaled Sudeep to follow him inside. The room contained a locker box, which the doctor opened to reveal the same 'MDD (MY_DREAM_DEVICE)' device, now equipped with a positivity level reading scale. Dr. RamSingh took the device and set it on the table. Both he and Sudeep sat down and put on the headphones. The positivity scale showed 25%.

*"Alright, before we enter 'Deep_dream,' we need to prepare your thoughts with a significant amount of positivity. This meter shows how much positive energy you have. Right now, you have 25% positivity, but to enter 'Deep_dream,' you need at least 50%. So, try to think positively. Recall something that made you joyful, something that brings you peace,"* Dr. RamSingh instructed.

*"Doctor, I'm trying. Every time I seek happiness, I end up pretending. Deep down, I know I'm not truly happy. My happiness never lasts long. Whenever I feel happy, those incidents, those tragedies come to mind"* Sudeep confessed.

Dr. RamSingh leaned forward, *"There's one universal truth about life: everything that happens is meant to happen, and we can't change the past by going back in time. The only thing we can do is accept the situation and move forward with a positive outlook."*

He continued, *"Let me share an incident that changed my life. As I told you before, I've done many things, including committing various crimes and serving multiple prison sentences."*

*"In a dimly lit prison, where shadows lingered as constant companions, there was an old man in the cell beside mine. His was the only cell with a small, narrow window—a gateway to a world I could not see. Every day, without fail, he would sit by that window and describe the outside world to me. His words painted vivid pictures of sprawling meadows, bustling towns, and skies that shifted from azure to amber at dusk. For five years, his voice was my*

lifeline, breaking the monotony of our confinement and filling my mind with beauty I had long forgotten.

At first, his stories were a source of joy and comfort. I hung on every word, imagining the sights and sounds he described. But as time passed, that joy soured into something darker. A seed of envy took root in my heart. Why should he have that window? Why should he alone see the world beyond these oppressive walls while I was left to rot in the dark? The thought consumed me, and his stories, once a balm to my weary soul, became a cruel reminder of what I lacked.

One night, I heard him coughing violently. The sound was harsh, desperate, like a drowning man gasping for air. I turned toward him and saw him clutching his chest, his frail body wracked with pain. His eyes met mine through the bars, wide with fear and pleading. He gestured weakly, urging me to call for the guards, to save him. For a moment, I hesitated, my heart pounding in my ears. But then, a darker thought crept into my mind—a thought that gripped me like a vice. If he were gone, his cell, his window, could be mine. I could finally see the world he spoke of.

So I stood there, rooted to the spot, and did nothing. I watched as his breaths grew shallower, his body trembling until it stilled completely. The silence that followed was deafening, and the weight of my choice pressed heavily on me. Yet, beneath the guilt, there was anticipation—a twisted sense of triumph. The window would be mine.

*The next day, I asked to be moved to his cell. My request was granted without question, and as I stepped inside, my pulse quickened. This was it—the moment I had longed for. I approached the window, my heart racing with anticipation. But when I looked out, my breath caught in my throat. There was no sprawling meadow, no bustling town, no golden skies. There was only the vast, unbroken expanse of the open ocean, stretching endlessly to the horizon."*

*"I realized he was creating happiness for himself by imagining things that never happened. I felt deep remorse. If I had called the guards, he might have lived a few more days, and I would have continued to enjoy his stories. That incident taught me the power of positive thinking and kindness. It changed my life, showing me that even small incidents can have a profound impact,"* Dr. RamSingh shared.

Sudeep felt a surge of positivity, and the scale showed 40%. But he also remembered the tragedies that had wrecked his life. *"Yes, like yours, an incident changed my life, but negatively. If Pallavi hadn't left me, I would have been happy,"* he said with grief.

Dr. RamSingh noticed the scale and realized Sudeep needed more encouragement. *"You think your life is dark because she left you, right? Remember, the sunrise comes after the darkest hours of the night, and stars shine brightest in the darkest skies. If you're facing darkness now, it means dawn is near, and your life will soon be beautiful."* He continued with more uplifting words, helping Sudeep cherish the positive aspects of his life. Sudeep envisioned a brighter future. He felt new, better, and more hopeful. The positivity resonated within him, and he smiled with newfound hope.

Dr. RamSingh sensed the shift in Sudeep's mindset. The positivity scale showed 50%. Before the effect diminished, he knew it was the perfect moment to move forward into 'Deep_dream.'

"Okay, let's get into 'Deep_dream'" Dr. RamSingh said promptly, switching on the device.

# VI

# Maadhavan Wake up!!! – Part 3

Maadhavan awakened on the bus, groggily observing that it had come to a halt. Abdullah, still trying to wake him up, and a samosa vendor shouting outside added to his disoriented state.

Rubbing his eyes, Maadhavan mumbled, *"Okay, okay... I'm awake."* He bought two plates of samosas. Taking a bite, he exclaimed, *"This is the best samosa I've ever had."* Abdullah smiled knowingly, *"I knew you'd say that. I felt the same."*

After fifteen minutes, the bus continued its journey. It moved smoothly until, abruptly, two police officers stopped it.

They boarded the bus, with one officer announcing, *"Don't panic. We have information that drugs are being smuggled on this bus, so please cooperate as we check your luggage."* Both officers began their search. Soon, they found drugs on the person seated in front of Maadhavan.

One officer dragged the trafficker off the bus. Relieved, Maadhavan and Abdullah were glad they wouldn't have to undergo a search.

However, the other officer approached Maadhavan and ordered him to pay a fine of five hundred rupees. Startled, Maadhavan stood up and protested, *"What... fine? For what reason? I didn't smuggle any drugs."* The officer replied, *"You are being fined for violating traffic rules."* Confused, Maadhavan asked, *"What? Officer, I'm on a bus, and I have a ticket. Why should I pay a fine?"* The officer responded, *"Brother, you must pay a fine of 500 rupees for not wearing your seatbelt."* Maadhavan laughed nervously, *"What? Seatbelts in a bus? But, officer, there are no..."* He turned to see that all the other passengers were wearing seatbelts. Shocked, he looked at Abdullah, who was also wearing a seatbelt. Baffled, Maadhavan muttered, *"But how? Buses don't have seatbelts..."*

Suddenly, Abdullah shouted, *"Wake up, Maadhavan... put the seatbelt on... wake up."* Maadhavan's pupils dilated. Realization dawned on him, and he smiled wryly, thinking, *"So, this is also a dream? I'm still sleeping somewhere..."*

Maadhavan awoke joyously in a car, with Abdullah shouting from the driver's seat, *"Wake up, Maadhavan... the cops are in front, wear your seatbelt."*

৪৩

**Half an hour earlier:**

The car cruised down the quiet, sun-dappled streets, its engine humming steadily. Abdullah was at the wheel, his hands firm but relaxed, guiding the vehicle effortlessly. Beside him sat Maadhavan, carefree and animated, tapping rhythmically on the car radio and breaking into impromptu, off-tune singing that filled the car with a lively air. The two friends were on a mission. In three months, a short film competition awaited at their college—a golden opportunity they were eager to seize.

Maadhavan, Abdullah, and their mutual friend Jeeva had decided to create something unforgettable. They were heading to Jeeva's house to shoot the first scene of their film. Excitement buzzed in the air, though the seriousness of the task hadn't yet dampened their jovial spirits.

As they drove, Abdullah glanced briefly at Maadhavan and asked, "*So, remind me again—what's the main theme of this masterpiece we're working on?*"

Maadhavan, leaning back with his signature nonchalance, yawned loudly before replying, "*It's about an insomniac patient and a psychiatrist who tries to cure him. Pretty deep, huh?*" He chuckled softly, though the yawn had drained some of his energy.

Abdullah nodded, his focus returning to the road. "*Sounds interesting,*" he said, his voice steady but tinged with curiosity.

"*Yeah, yeah,*" Maadhavan muttered, waving dismissively. His earlier enthusiasm had waned, replaced by the irresistible pull of sleep. "*Okay, let me catch a nap. Wake me up when we get to Jeeva's place,*" he added, loosening his seatbelt for comfort.

"*Sure,*" Abdullah replied, his eyes fixed ahead as the sunlight flickered through the trees lining the road.

Maadhavan shifted in his seat, leaning his head against the window. The steady rhythm of the car's motion lulled him, and his eyelids grew heavier by the second. Within moments, the chatter and hum around him faded into a tranquil silence. He was asleep, leaving Abdullah alone with the quiet road and the murmuring thoughts of the film they were about to bring to life.

• 27 •

# VII
## Deep Dream

Sudeep lay sound asleep on his bed, lost in a world of dreams, when a flurry of movement broke through the stillness. His faithful Pomeranian, Chan, bounded into the room with uncontainable energy. The little dog leaped onto the bed, his fluffy paws landing softly on Sudeep's chest. With a flurry of wet licks, Chan's excitement was contagious—he knew it was time for their daily walk.

Sudeep stirred, groaning slightly as he opened his eyes to see Chan's wagging tail and wide, expectant eyes. He chuckled and ruffled Chan's fur affectionately. *"Alright, alright, I'm up!"* he said, stretching lazily as he swung his legs over the side of the bed.

After freshening up, Sudeep grabbed Chan's collar and leash. But the little rascal had other plans. Chan darted around playfully, evading every attempt to secure the collar. *"Hold still, you troublemaker!"* Sudeep laughed, exasperated yet amused. After several failed attempts, he finally managed to fasten the collar. *"Shall we go?"* he asked teasingly, and Chan responded with an excited bark, as if to say, What are we waiting for?

Sudeep grabbed a packet of biscuits and a water bottle before stepping outside with Chan. The joy in the air was palpable, the bond between them unspoken yet deeply felt.

Fifteen minutes later, they arrived at the park. The sun filtered through the trees, casting dappled patterns on the ground. Sudeep found a bench and sat down, while Chan sprawled contentedly at his feet. Pulling out the biscuits, Sudeep placed a few on the ground. Chan devoured them eagerly, his wagging tail a constant blur of happiness.

As Sudeep watched Chan eat, a wave of gratitude washed over him. He felt lucky to have such a loyal companion, one who brought joy to even the dullest of days. When the biscuits were gone, Chan let out a small bark, pleading for more. Sudeep shook his head with a smile. *"That's all for today, buddy. Let's head home."*

On their way back, a vibrant butterfly fluttered into their path. Chan's ears perked up instantly, and with a sudden burst of energy, he leaped toward it, snapping playfully at the air. The butterfly danced away, and Chan gave chase, tugging hard on the leash. Sudeep struggled to keep hold but couldn't match the dog's determination. With a final, forceful pull, Chan broke free, bolting after the elusive butterfly.

*"Chan! Stop!"* Sudeep shouted, panic creeping into his voice. He sprinted after his dog, his heart pounding, but Chan was too fast. The butterfly veered left, and Chan followed, disappearing around a corner. Sudeep stopped, breathless and defeated, shouting Chan's name into the void. The silence that followed was unbearable.

He returned home, alone and heartbroken. The once lively house now felt empty. Days passed, but the ache in his chest remained. Sudeep couldn't eat or sleep, consumed by thoughts of his beloved Chan. What will he eat? Where will he sleep? How will he survive? The questions tormented him, each one heavier than the last.

Two days later, a knock at the door shattered the oppressive silence. Sudeep rushed to open it, his heart pounding with cautious hope. Standing there was a young woman, holding a dirt-covered but familiar bundle.

"*Chan!*" Sudeep cried as his dog leaped into his arms, licking his face frantically. Tears streamed down Sudeep's face as he clung to his furry companion, overwhelmed with relief and gratitude.

The girl smiled gently. "*I found him near my house. His collar had your name and address, so I brought him back.*"

Sudeep looked at her with teary eyes. "*Thank you so much... What's your name?*"

"*Pallavi,*" she replied with a kind smile.

From that day, Pallavi became a frequent presence in Sudeep's life. Their bond grew stronger, and eventually, love blossomed between them. One day, Sudeep nervously proposed to Pallavi over the phone. To his delight, she said yes and asked him to meet her at their usual park.

But as Sudeep waited there for two hours, anxiety began to gnaw at him. He called her, only to hear an unfamiliar voice—a nurse informing him that Pallavi had been in a car accident and was in the hospital.

Racing to the hospital, Sudeep's heart pounded with fear. He found the doctor and begged for news. "*She's out of danger,*" the doctor said, "*but there's a significant chance of memory loss.*"

The words hit Sudeep like a punch to the gut. His legs trembled as he asked, "*Can I see her?*"

After a series of tests, the doctors discovered a minor tumor in Pallavi's brain. Though alarming, it was treatable. "*The accident may have saved her life,*" the doctor explained.

*"If the tumor had gone unnoticed, it could have been fatal."*

The surgery was successful, but when Pallavi woke up, she stared blankly at Sudeep. She didn't recognize him. The past two years, including their love story, had been erased from her memory.

Sudeep stood in the doorway, his heart breaking. Tears welled up in his eyes, but through the pain, a flicker of hope remained. The accident, though tragic, had given her a second chance at life. He whispered, *"I'll wait for you, Pallavi"* before walking away, his cheeks wet with tears and a bittersweet smile on his face.

Sudeep woke up in the LUCID room, still connected to the My_Dream device with the positivity reading scale. His eyes glittered with tears as he removed the headphones. Dr. RamSingh also removed his headphones and checked the positivity meter, which showed 92%. Placing their headphones on the table, the doctor asked Sudeep how he felt. *"Mixed emotions—sad, but happy,"* Sudeep replied with a smile.

Dr. RamSingh was pleased with the change in Sudeep and said, *"That's what I expected. Life is exactly what you just dreamed— a mix of difficulties, tragedies, and happiness. There is always a ray of light at the end of the dark tunnel. After every hardship, there is a happy life ahead, and all you can do is hope for it."* Sudeep listened intently, still under the dream's impact, and realized he must hope for a better future.

The doctor then introduced the second exercise: *"From today, start writing your life's journal."* Sudeep was unclear and asked, *"What is a life's journal? You mean a diary?"* The doctor replied, *"Yes, like a diary, but you must also write the positive and negative outcomes of each incident and what you learned from it."* Sudeep promised to start writing the journal before bed.

Dr. RamSingh also advised Sudeep to spend ten to twenty minutes each day as a 'worry period' to think about the bad things that happened. Sudeep doubted this would help, as he spent all night worrying about his life. The doctor assured him, *"Yes, it will make a big difference. This simple habit has helped many people recover from depression. You must do this daily. I think this session is enough for today. Let's return to reality."*

# VIII
# Maadhavan!!! - Watch out...

Maadhavan stirred awake in the passenger seat, his friend Abdullah's voice slicing through the haze of sleep. *"Maadhavan! Seatbelt! Now!"* Abdullah yelled, urgency etched into his tone.

Startled, Maadhavan scrambled to fasten his seatbelt, the click of the buckle echoing just as they rolled past a group of stern-faced policemen. For a tense moment, the car remained under scrutiny, but the officers waved them through without a second glance.

Abdullah exhaled audibly, his laughter breaking the silence. *"Phew! That was close. Luckily, we didn't get caught!"* Maadhavan joined in with a relieved chuckle. *"Yeah, or they would've definitely fined us for not wearing seatbelts."*

Abdullah laughed harder, his amusement tinged with mischief. *"Not just for seatbelts. If they'd stopped us, I'd have been fined for something worse—driving without a license!"*

The laughter caught in Maadhavan's throat as he froze, his expression morphing from humor to disbelief. *"Wait, what? You don't have a driving license?"*

Abdullah's grin widened, unfazed. *"Not yet. I applied for a learner's license just yesterday."*

Maadhavan's jaw dropped, and he mockingly clasped his hands together in prayer. *"God, please let us reach Jeeva's house without harming anyone or anything,"* he said, half-joking and half-serious.

A comfortable silence settled over them for a few minutes, broken only by the hum of the engine and the rhythm of the tires against the road. Eventually, Maadhavan broke the quiet, recounting his vivid, bizarre dream. "I had the strangest dream. It started raining inside my house, and then I was suddenly in school where our principal was selling samosas. And when I thought it couldn't get weirder, I woke up in a bus where the police fined me for not wearing a seatbelt!"

Abdullah listened, a crooked smile playing on his lips. *"Seriously? That entire epic in such a short nap? You must be the world's fastest dreamer."*

Before Maadhavan could respond, Abdullah's phone rang, its jarring tone breaking their flow. Abdullah kept his eyes on the road as he handed it to Maadhavan. *"Check who it is,"* he said.

Maadhavan glanced at the screen. *"It's Jeeva,"* he announced, answering the call.

On the other end, Jeeva's voice was brisk. *"Where are you guys? How much longer?"*

Maadhavan peered at the passing scenery. *"Another 10 to 15 minutes,"* he assured Jeeva.

As he spoke, the phone slipped from his grip and tumbled to the car floor. *"Hold on"* Maadhavan said, leaning forward to retrieve it. The world seemed to shift in that moment. As Maadhavan sat upright again, phone in hand, his eyes widened in alarm. A man was walking along the edge of the road, dangerously close to their path.

*"Watch out!"* Maadhavan yelled, his voice sharp with fear.

Abdullah snapped his focus back to the road. His hands gripped the steering wheel as he spotted the man directly in their path. He stomped on the brakes, the tires screeching in protest, but momentum was a cruel master. The sound of the collision was deafening, a sickening thud as the car struck the man. The vehicle jerked to a halt, silence rushing in like a tidal wave, broken only by the rapid, panicked breaths of the two friends.

For a moment, neither of them moved, the weight of what had just happened pressing down on them like a stormcloud ready to burst.

# IX
## Climax

Sudeep and Dr. RamSingh woke up on the sofa where they were connected to the 'MDD (MY_DREAM_DEVICE)'. They both removed their headphones and set them aside. Dr. RamSingh got up and went into the kitchen, while Sudeep recalled everything that happened in the dream, feeling slightly dizzy. The doctor returned with a glass of water and handed it to Sudeep, who drank it and placed the glass on the teapoy. *"Come on, let's go for a walk,"* the doctor suggested. Rubbing his forehead, Sudeep agreed, *"Yeah, sure, I need some fresh air too."*

Dr. RamSingh grabbed his diary, switched off the lights and fan, locked the front door, and they walked outside into the street.

It was around 12:30 PM. Both of them walked along the side of the road, with trees lining both sides. The doctor enjoyed the nature around them, holding his closed diary, while Sudeep felt a slight relief from the dizziness. *"Do you feel better?"* the doctor asked.

Sudeep replied that he felt a bit better but was still slightly dizzy. The doctor reassured him that the dizziness would subside within 10 to 15 minutes, just as it had for him the first time he used the 'MDD'. As predicted, after 10 minutes, Sudeep felt completely relieved.

*"So, how was the therapy?"* the doctor inquired. Sudeep was unsure if the therapy had worked but acknowledged it felt different from previous treatments. *"It was really intense. What you said in the dream was similar to what other doctors told me, but this time it felt different."*

The doctor smiled, *"The difference you felt is because of the dream. As I mentioned earlier, an idea in a dream has a more significant impact than in reality."* Sudeep then asked if this therapy would be sufficient to cure him. The doctor replied, *"The impact of the dream will last long, but we need to see the progress. Do the breathing exercises, journal writing, and worry period for one month. If the sleeplessness doesn't reduce, we might need deeper dream sessions. If it does, continue the exercises. Besides that, read books, listen to music, and raise a pet if you're comfortable. Dogs, for example, are the only beings that love us more than themselves. Love is the best medicine I can prescribe to you."*

They walked in silence for a while. Dr. RamSingh leafed through his diary, recalling past incidents. Sudeep broke the silence, asking why the doctor stopped giving therapies. The doctor remained silent for a few seconds before closing his diary. *"Many doctors thought my treatment methods were risky and raised their voices against me. The government canceled my license without hearing my justification."*

Curious, Sudeep asked, *"Why did they think your methods were dangerous? Is it related to that hospital fire accident?"* The doctor nodded, *"Yes, but I didn't cause the fire. My student did. He used 'MDD' without fully understanding it. He learned how to enter and create the surroundings but didn't know how to exit the dream. When he returned to reality, he confused it with the dream and tried to escape it. He thought killing himself in the dream would bring him back to reality."*

Sudeep understood and said, *"So, he set himself and the whole hospital on fire."* He felt sorry for the doctor and his student, asking, *"Then what happened next?"*

The doctor replied with anguish, *"They seized my license, criticized my methods, and banned 'MDD' devices."*

They continued the walk in silence for few minutes then Sudeep looked at the doctor with curiosity, his voice tinged with both hesitation and concern as he asked, "What about you, Doctor? What are your plans for the future?"

The doctor paused, a faint, bittersweet smile tugging at the corners of his lips. His eyes, filled with a mix of weariness and unspoken sorrow, drifted to a distant point as though searching for something lost. *"Plans?"* he said softly, his voice carrying the weight of years lived and battles fought. *"I have none. I'll just wait... wait for my death."*

Sudeep felt a pang in his chest, the stark simplicity of those words leaving an ache in the air between them. Yet, before he could respond, the doctor's gaze softened, a flicker of warmth breaking through the shadows. *"But I do have a desire,"* he continued, his voice growing wistful.

"When I was with my family," the doctor began, his tone tinged with nostalgia, *"we used to visit the beach. It was our favorite place—where the horizon seemed endless, and the waves carried our laughter away with them."* His lips trembled slightly as he continued, his voice cracking under the weight of the memory.

*"One day, I lay on the sand, staring at the vast blue sky. My son, with the brightest grin, pointed upward and shouted, 'Look, Papa! A rainbow!' It stretched across the sky, vivid and magical. At that exact moment, my daughter squealed with excitement, 'A shooting star! Papa, make a wish!' Their voices, their joy... I*

*can still hear them as if it were yesterday."*

The doctor paused, closing his eyes as if trying to hold on to the fragments of that precious moment. His voice trembled, barely above a whisper, as he said, *"Their laughter... their happiness... they were my rainbow and my shooting stars. They lit up my life in ways I never deserved."*

A heavy silence filled the room, punctuated only by the faint sound of Sudeep's breathing as he listened intently, his own emotions caught in the gravity of the doctor's words.

*"Before I leave this world,"* the doctor said, his eyes opening but still fixed on that unseen horizon, *"I wish to relive that moment—or something close to it. I want to see a rainbow and a shooting star together. Just once. Just one more time."*

His voice faltered, and he exhaled deeply, as though unburdening his soul. *"It may sound foolish, but that's my wish... my only wish."*

He then asked Sudeep, *"Do you have any desires like that?"*

Sudeep replied, *"No, not like that. But I have a goal: to start my own construction company called Sparrow Constructions."*

The doctor felt happy and said, *"I hope your dream comes true one day."*

A few minutes later, unexpectedly, black clouds covered the sunny sky, and it started to drizzle. Before it rained heavily, they decided to head back. As they returned, the clouds spread out, and the sun shone on their path. The doctor looked up and saw a beautiful rainbow next to the sun. He instantly told Sudeep to see the seven-colored semicircle. They were mesmerized by the view when suddenly they heard a vehicle speeding towards them. They looked straight and saw a car approaching uncontrollably. Before they could react, the car collided with the doctor, throwing him five feet away.

Sudeep stood still in shock, unable to react. Everything happened so quickly. The doctor, who almost cured him, lay bleeding on the road, struggling to lift his head. Sudeep ran towards him, lifted his head, and placed it on his lap, noticing his hands were covered in blood. The doctor was watching the rainbow with no pain on his face. Sudeep's eyes filled with tears, and as a drop fell on the doctor's head, he noticed Sudeep crying.

*"Don't cry,"* the doctor said in a struggling husky voice. Sudeep responded, *"It's all because of me. If I hadn't come to you, this wouldn't have happened. I'm sorry..."*

The car stopped immediately after hitting the doctor. Maadhavan and Abdullah got out and approached them. They noticed the doctor was still alive. *"He's alive,"* Maadhavan said. Sudeep shouted, *"Call an ambulance."* Abdullah ran to the car, took his phone, and dialed 108.

The doctor called Sudeep closer and said, *"Don't try to save me. I'm finally going to meet my kids and wife. Let me die."* Sudeep cried, *"Don't do this to me, doctor. Don't die on me."* The doctor signaled Sudeep to bring his diary. Sudeep reached for it, and Maadhavan helped him take it. Sudeep gave it to the doctor, who handed it back to Sudeep. *"After we die, the only thing we leave behind is our memories. Don't let my memories die. Remember me till your last breath,"* the doctor said.

Sudeep replied, *"I will. I won't forget you till I die."*

While watching the sky, the doctor smiled peacefully and asked Sudeep to look up. Sudeep and Maadhavan lifted their heads and saw the rainbow and two shooting stars falling. *"See... shooting stars. What a delightful view..."* the doctor said, forgetting his pain.

*"On the first page, there's a poem my wife told me once. Will you read it for me?"* the doctor asked. Sudeep opened the

diary and was amazed. He turned all the pages but found nothing except two words on each page. The doctor asked Maadhavan to come closer. *"That was a beautiful climax. Don't forget this after you wake up,"* he said. Maadhavan was shocked and heard a bass tone in his mind—it was his mobile's ringtone. In shock, he realized he was still dreaming. Sudeep read the two words in the doctor's diary loudly, *"Wake up..."*

# X
# Epilogue

Maadhavan woke up in his room—still, it was raining heavily, so the electricity hadn't come back. He leaned forward from the wall and noticed his phone ringing next to the script papers. He picked it up and saw that Abdullah was calling. Simultaneously, he heard someone knocking on the door. As he answered the call and walked towards the door, he said, *"Hello?"*

His friend Abdullah replied, *"Open the door!"* Maadhavan opened it to find Abdullah and Jeeva standing outside. Abdullah had a large bag in his hand, which he handed over to Maadhavan as they both came inside. Closing the door, Maadhavan asked, *"You got everything?"* while rummaging through the bag.

*"Yeah, we bought everything you asked for,"* Abdullah replied, then asked, *"Were you asleep? We were knocking for almost five minutes."*

Maadhavan took out the costumes, wigs, and everything from the bag. *"Yeah, I fell asleep. I'm sorry, I didn't hear you knocking,"* he said while trying on the costumes.

Jeeva, holding a packet of samosas, placed it on the bed. He took one out and, while eating, looked at the script. Noticing that the ending wasn't complete, he asked, *"What about the climax? Did you get any ideas?"*

After donning the costume, Maadhavan glanced in the mirror and was surprised. He looked exactly like Dr. RamSingh. Remembering the entire dream about Sudeep and Dr. RamSingh, he said, *"Yeah, I have one. And this ending is going to be perfect. I'm sure we'll win that competition for sure"* Maadhavan replied to Jeeva with a confident smile on his face.